-<u>Midnight Playground</u>-
A Collected Anthology of Original Short Stories

Table of Contents

Garrett K. Jones

GKJ Publishing
2024

-Acknowledgements-

Thank you to the triune God who created my inmost being and saved me. I do what I do because you created me in Your likeness with a passion for creativity just like you. Thank you for the gift of storytelling you have given to me; help me to use it well.

Thank you to my family – my parents, my brother, and my son – for loving and supporting me. Thanks especially to my mother for constantly keeping me encouraged in the work I do to further my craft. I love and appreciate all you do for me.

Thank you to my fellow writers and friends with whom I've connected over the last few years. Your encouragement and conversations have kept me from losing sight of my enjoyment for what I write.

Lastly, thank you to NYC Midnight and Writer's Playground for the opportunity to create some really fun stories even if I didn't go all the way and win an award. I've appreciated the surge in creativity you have generated within me from the awesome prompts and challenges.

To the readers, thank you for your support. I write as much for you as I do for myself.

For Logan. Love, Dad.

-Introduction-

Writing, telling stories, and entertaining people has been my lifelong dream. Over the course of the last ten years, I have done what I can to make that dream a reality through self-publishing works of fiction and poetry meant to entertain and – maybe – inspire others to try their hand at something new and creative. I can't tell you the number of times I've been at an event to promote my books and I've encountered one or more people who aren't just looking for a new title to entertain them, they're looking for encouragement... almost to the point of asking for permission to tell whatever story they harbor deep inside their hearts.

I wouldn't be where I am if I hadn't received encouragement. I had people in my life, - family, friends, and mentors – who read my work and provided me with constructive criticism and tips for getting my stories published. And while I've published several titles, I have encountered my moments where I've wanted and needed to produce something new but haven't been able because I hit some kind of mental block. I've started and stopped projects, but things just don't stick.

After the release of the fifth book in my fantasy series, I immediately got to work writing the sixth installment. I was midway through Chapter 16 when I suddenly found myself without the impetus to write... the creative flow dammed up and I haven't really been as productive as I would have preferred.

But to break through that wall – or at least circumvent it – I began participating in a number of writing competitions over the last couple of years. Most of the competitions have been held by NYC Midnight, a short story competition organization based out of New York. Their 250- and 500-word challenges have tested my ability to say more with less, to focus on stronger word choices rather than long, drawn out prose. The other organization I've recently become connected with is Writer's Playground, which is also based on the east coast. I signed up for their short story competition which challenged me to write a short story (up to 3000 words) in ten days.

These challenges have been instrumental in getting my creative flow back. In particular, the story I wrote for Writer's Playground was the single longest piece of storytelling I've written in more than a year that didn't involve transposing something handwritten into a document file or starting and stopping a project for months on end, or just flat out giving up. And as I shared some of my shorter pieces with a relative, it was recommended I organize them into a published collection. I stewed on the suggestion for several weeks, and ended up taking it to heart. Thus "Midnight Playground" is the result, taking the title from the two major organizations with which I've been participating.

What follows are the stories written for those very competitions, plus some other stories that were created for other reasons. I have them broken down by category, with the 250-word and 500-word stories up front to provide snippets of concise storytelling as a means of whetting the appetite before giving readers the larger main dishes of more detailed fiction. The stories range in genre from romantic comedy to ghost story, from science fiction to cosmic horror, and everything in between.

I hope you enjoy what is to come and that it entertains – and maybe – inspires you to be creative in your own way.

-GKJ

-Part 1-
250

-Cocoa & a Shared Kiss-

An embarrassed giggle followed Sarah's shriek.

"Got you," Grant smiled, catching her before she fell onto the ice.

"I can't do this," Sarah said.

"You're not going to ace this on the first try."

"You are."

Grant's grin only widened.

"What," Sarah asked.

Grant hung his head sheepishly.

"When I said I hadn't been skating, I meant at this rink," he said.

"Why didn't you just tell me?"

"I wanted to do this for the first time together."

Sarah stared into his eyes, studying them. His green irises locked with her mesmerizing amber hues as she brushed a brunette tress from her face. She shivered, the cozy outdoor location's ambiance juxtaposed by the winter chill.

"Okay, then what should I do," she asked.

Grant stood in front of her, facing against the other skaters' flow moving around them. He took her hands and slowly skated in reverse.

"Softly push off with your back foot," he said, encouraging her.

She did and started gliding.

"Okay, keep your back straight like you're walking and slide your feet instead of stepping."

Sarah moved her right leg as instructed, followed by her left.

"Focus on me," Grant said.

The pair slowly finished two laps around the rink before Grant skated beside her, their fingers interlaced. Sarah chanced a look at him, returning his infectious smile. She hugged his arm affectionately three laps later, safe in his hold.

Their first *real* date ended an hour later over cups of steaming cocoa and a shared kiss.

-Sardines-

My hands fidgeted with anxious tensing as they clasped my knees to my chest. Trickles of sweat ran across my palms. My nerves sparked like miniature lightning bursts, an adrenaline-infused staccato impatiently burning through my bloodstream. My heart thudded in my chest, threatening to burst from my ribcage like one of the monsters Sigourney Weaver fought in the movies.

The tainted memory of watching "Aliens" with dad forced me to remember that I hid inside the closet's pitch-black darkness, buried under the bottom utility shelf behind a set of boxes and an old cannister Hoover. A shiver forced my back to arch and I smacked my head against the shelf bottom with a dull thump. I paused, hoping my pursuers hadn't heard me.

The closet door swung open, answering my prayers; I never even heard the unlubricated doorknob turn nor the seeker's footsteps clopping on the wood flooring outside the space. Bright light streamed from the seeker's flashlight.

I only saw feet clad in worn black high-tops, the laces double-knotted. I held my breath, refusing to exhale for fear of betraying myself. I counted the seconds until the seeker switched off the torch, closed the door, and walked off...

It was an eternity.

The seeker carefully hid his footfalls from my ears, continuing the search.

I stealthily moved from my nook and placed my ear to the door. I heard nothing. I finally sighed and ran towards the east end of the house. The seekers *never* found me.

I won.

-Locking Up-

Amanda shivered. The library interior froze. Her breath turned into foggy gasps as darkness permeated the children's reading room. A prickling tingled across her back, centering on her left shoulder. Her heart skipped a beat at the invisible contact.

She shelved recently returned titles when the power died. Her coworkers had already gone home and she finished locking up.

"Will you read to us," whispered voices said behind her.

Amanda looked over her shoulder, plucking her phone from her pocket.

Only stygian blackness loomed, its span saturating everything. Had she actually heard something?

Her phone had no service, the signal blocked by the century-old construction.

"Please," the childlike voices urged. "We promise we'll be good."

Amanda faced the room's far corner where a puppet theater sat. She tentatively approached, the buzz of the fluorescent lighting vainly trying to return. The ballasts flickered erratically. She hugged herself, terror shrinking her the closer she got.

Teddy bears floated on their own, dancing through the puppet stage as disembodied giggling echoed in the space.

"Don't hurt us. We'll be good."

Fear filled the voices. Children sobbed.

"Get out," a new, monstrous voice screeched.

A slender figure appeared, etched from the hard shadows. It stared at her. She knew him, recognizing the face from the library founder's portrait hanging menacingly above the circulation desk. He died eighty years earlier, but here he stood with a knife in hand.

Eobard Jacobs – a closeted murderer – lilted towards her, slashing the spectral blade with an inhuman shriek.

-Unfinished Business-

"Shit!"

Greg sprinted down the church's north wing, trying to keep a healthy distance between himself and *whatever the hell* that thing was.

He planned on rescheduling his janitorial night shift availability after this.

He wished he hadn't even come in tonight.

Not even an hour into his shift, he heard humming inside the main women's restroom. It sounded like the HVAC system's shrillness, which often whistled when the air pressure forced the door ajar. He almost missed it over the tune coming from his earbuds.

He investigated.

A spectral entity suspended in midair in front of the mirror on the bathroom's far side.

He gawked.

The ethereal silver presence faced him.

He slipped to the floor as it quickly lunged for him.

It drew closer, ghostly hands reaching.

He got up and ran to the far end of the west lobby and turned the corner. He panted hard, his heart hammering his sternum.

The emergency lighting died, replaced by solid darkness and shimmering white.

It rounded the corner, following him.

"You," it howled.

That's when Greg ran through the north wing, closing every classroom door behind him. The argent glow faded and disappeared as he passed through the nursery and reached the kids' lobby.

He looked over his shoulder, seeing nothing following him.

He breathed a sigh of relief, hoping the pastor might believe him *this* time.

He turned towards the glass doors.

The entity hovered inches away

"You," it hissed.

The light faded.

Greg never finished his shift.

-Part 2-
500

-Pregnancy Brain-

"Where's the ice cream scoop," Paul called across the apartment.

"It should be in the utensil drawer," Beth replied.

Paul opened the shallow drawer where they kept a grilling fork, a pair of tongs, several measuring cups, the detachable beaters for their electric hand mixer, and a few other cooking tools. But he couldn't find the one thing he needed and the container of chocolate gelato from the nearby grocery store was quickly thawing in the summer heat.

"It's not here," he said.

"Because you never put anything back where it's supposed to go," Beth complained.

"Are you kidding?! I'm the only one who puts things back where they go."

"But you don't do it right."

"How many different ways is there to put an ice cream scoop into a utensil drawer," he asked.

Beth, four months pregnant with their first child, walked into the kitchen from the front room.

"You'd be surprised," she replied, giving him a kiss on the lips.

"Try me," he said, reciprocating her affection.

"Let me see how you do it."

"I'm pretty sure you know how I do it," he jibed as he rubbed her stomach.

She playfully pushed him away and repeated her request, pursing her lips and crinkling her brow in that adorable way that made him fall in love with her all over again. He picked up a spatula from the countertop drying rack and placed it in the basket near the stove holding the other spatulas and cooking spoons.

"Impressive," Beth said. "Do it again."

Paul selected a clean saucepan and placed it neatly into the cupboard under the stove where it fit between a larger pan and a smaller pan like a set of Russian nesting dolls.

"I love it when you think you know what you're doing," she commented.

Paul rolled his eyes and grabbed a tablespoon from the drying rack, using it to scoop gelato into his bowl.

"Really," Beth asked.

"I'll use the right tool when you tell me where you've hidden it."

"Where *I've* hidden it?!"

"Yeah," Paul said. "You've been misplacing a ton of stuff lately. I think your sister called it 'pregnancy brain.'"

"I *don't* have pregnancy brain."

"Oh yeah? Where did I find the TV remote the other day?

"I don't know, Paul... I don't remember."

Paul smiled.

"You left it in your sock drawer when you were getting your shoes on to go for a walk."

"I did not," Beth exclaimed, her cheeks flushing with embarrassment.

"You did."

"Well... you... you accidentally left your coffee mug in the bathroom."

"You're right, I did," Paul said. "Totally my fault."

"Don't agree with me," Beth said. "It's not fair."

"Sure it is," Paul said, kissing his wife as the phone rang.

He moved to answer it.

"Hon?"

"Yeah," Beth replied.

Paul pointed. The pair stared at the missing ice cream scoop sitting in the phone's charging cradle.

"Beth, where's the phone?"

Beth inhaled sharply.

"I might have a little pregnancy brain," she said.

-Sarah & the Fae-

Not all fairy tales are happy stories.

Sarah stooped at the faint depression in the lawn stretching out along Richmond Green as an armored figure demolished The Prince's Head pub. The chilly November air hung heavy, laden by the wanton desire to release the smallest inkling of precipitation. A light dew managed to materialize against the finely cut grass shards. She remembered listening to the shrill whistle of the train from Wales to England, the *chug-chug* and *klikity-klak* of the metal wheels her mantra during the four hours she spent riding the rails across the United Kingdom.

She spent two weeks in Swansea before this, pursuing a nasty Púca terrorizing attendees at the Plantasia Tropical Zoo. The shapeshifting hobgoblin repeatedly transformed into a goat or horse and took visitors on wild, concussion-inducing rides across the zoo grounds if they made contact with the creature's back. As the little beastie put it, "It was just a bit of mischief in honor of Samhain". Sarah entered the zoo with a pair of silver spurs attached to her worn leather combat boots, driving them into the Púca's sides to control it before casting the banishment charm.

Before that, Sarah wrestled with a far more malicious creature in Inverness, Scotland. The Kelpie swimming in the loch began hunting on the night of the autumnal equinox, signifying the three days of Mabon. It swam from Inverness to Drumnadrochit to Invermoriston to Fort Augustus and back, dragging unwitting victims into the frigid, dark water to feed on them. Sarah's banishment charm wouldn't stop it, resulting in her shooting and killing it with a silver bullet.

Sarah briefly glimpsed the butterfly-shaped impression in the park grass. The wings' upper lobes extended into sharp, angular points like that of Elf ears. The Fae's mark, its entry point from its own realm into the mortal plain, still glowed with vibrant magic. She needed to kill it or the gateway wouldn't close.

The movies and cartoons never got it right; the Fae didn't just look like miniature humans with butterfly wings. They took on a plethora of forms, most commonly something vaguely Human-like when walking among mortals. And they certainly weren't benevolent visitors. Sarah hadn't planned on encountering another creature so soon after Wales. She called Richmond home and she planned to meet some friends at the pub before heading to a football match, but the portal opened in front of her and only she knew how to kill it.

She drew a nine-inch-long, iron-bladed knife from her travel pack and lunged at the figure attempting to slaughter a family of five with a golden sword glowing like sunlight. She caught it just under the ribs, in a place unprotected by its cuirass. Purple blood oozed from the wound as the iron burned pale flesh.

"You dare," the Fae hissed.

It lashed out at her but Sarah ducked under the uncoordinated swing. She dodged once more and plunged her knife into its throat. The Fae gurgled and dropped. Its gateway sealed.

-Ancestry-

Magic exploded, demolishing the brick wall protecting me from the battle raging throughout the cathedral's ruins.

"Mierda santa," I exclaimed, falling and twisting my ankle.

Nobody knew the portal between earth and Byd Hud opened until the elves revealed their secret civilization twenty years later, claiming peaceful intentions after decades of isolation. Magic poured from their world, giving ordinary humans access to a variety of new powers and abilities.

The war began fifty years later and it's been raging for nearly four times as long.

The Elves protracted the conflict; their prolonged lifespans and prevalent magic made them unstoppable when our modern technology failed in the presence of their powers.

"Where are you hiding, *hanner brid*," an accented voice lilted.

I breathed heavily, quietly grunting.

"Curare el tobillo," I whispered, channeling magic at my injury.

I heard boots crunching in the Sagrada Familia's rubble..

"Just like a *ci ast* to cower," the voice taunted. "You must be brave if you want to claim *Dail Gwyrdd* blood."

I ignored the taunting as it grew closer.

"Stand and face me."

I looked at my ankle; the bruising faded and pain ebbed. I glanced the elven voice's direction, catching my haggard reflection in a polished metal plate. My usually neatly trimmed brown hair hung unkempt in my face. I tucked it behind my ears, their tapered points more obvious now.

I never knew my father's lineage blended with the elves not long after they made their way to earth.

"Vés... vés... és aquí dins!"

New shouting.

The Mando de Operaciones Especiales found me. Spain's Army special forces hunted me in the middle of the war as soon as my identity flagged in their system.

"On és el mestis," I heard a human soldier ask. "Where is the half-breed?"

The Spanish government made elf ancestry illegal. My own neighbors and school friends betrayed me after my ears changed on my twelfth birthday. The prejudiced invaders hated human blood tainting their lineages just as much and set a bounty on my head, attracting the hunter pursuing me now. After five years of running, I was ready to-

"*Dyna chi,*" the accented voice exclaimed.

The elf raised a silver dagger, readying her attack.

"Dispara a l'elf!!!"

The soldiers' staccato burst of gunfire deafened the enclosed space. The she-elf cut the men down one by one, hacking arms and hands from each of them.

"Objectiu adquirit," I heard someone say behind me.

I turned around; another soldier aimed a rifle at me. I instinctively raised my hands.

"Derretir el arma," I shouted; the gun and its ammunition liquified in his hands just before the lone pursuer ended his life and pointed the tip of her blade at my throat.

"You are mine," she said.

Perdóname madre, I thought, closing my eyes.

"Daga, mata a tu amo," I sighed, breaking a promise I once made to my mother before she died.

The dagger leapt from the elf's grip, spun, and plunged halfway to the hilt in her breast.

-Nine-To-Five-

Rory's alarm – which sounded like a rooster crowing at the wee rays of dawn – erupted from the clock sitting on his bedside table.

"Feckin' cock of an alarm clock," he muttered.

He climbed out of bed and padded to the loo, relieved himself, then headed for the shower.

He performed his morning ablutions, careful to cover his wings to prevent water damage. He hated being exposed to water, but work required him to bathe at least every couple of days to keep his job.

Rory made the uphill trudge to the office, making sure to wear his overcoat to avoid the autumn downpour. He ate a berry scone and sipped his way-too-hot tea while on foot, burning the roof of his mouth and losing half his breakfast to the rather aggressive pigeon that always seemed to harass him on a daily basis.

"Oh, come on," he exclaimed as the fat bird landed on his arm, pilfered his scone, and flew off. "Me mam baked that jus' fer me!!!"

He arrived at his cubicle at Murphy, O'Brien, & Walsh LLC with five minutes before he needed to punch in.

"Oh, goody," he muttered. "I'm on time."

"Yer late," Duncan Walsh reamed him from above the partition blocking Rory's view of rest of the thirteenth floor.

"It's eight-fifty-five," Rory exclaimed. "I don't punch in until nine!"

Walsh – Rory's immediate supervisor in statistical analysis and data reconfiguration – glanced at the expensive silver watch on his left wrist.

"I'll be damned," Walsh said. "Well, don't be late."

Walsh walked off, leaving Rory to clock in and get to work.

"Hey," Rory's co-worker Michael said from the neighboring cubicle.

"Hey," Rory replied despondently. "You ever wonder why we're here?"

"Yeah, man," Michael said. "It's one of those great cosmic questions, and if I'm bein' hon-"

"No, you eejit, I mean why are we here... right now... workin' fer these twats?!"

Michael looked around, eyes wide at the outburst. Walsh remained oblivious as he chatted up the ginger lass on the other side of the floor.

"Why don't you tell me how you really feel," he said.

"I jus' don't see what the point o' all this busy work," Rory commented.

"It's gotta be done, mate," Michael said before returning to his work.

The day yawned ahead of Rory as he completed every menial task on the to-do list Walsh slacked to him. He spent lunch in the park across from the office, pretty certain the same damn pigeon from earlier stared at him, waiting for the opening to steal Rory's lunch. Someone nearby made an offhanded comment about Rory being a "salamander", slang for fire fairies.

"Feck 'em," Rory said to himself as he finished his sandwich and coffee and headed back indoors.

Walsh met him as he returned to his cubicle, waiting with a clipboard in hand.

"So I'm going to need you to work overtime tonight," the overpaid human said.

"That. Does. It," Rory exclaimed.

He ignited his cubicle with magic and quit.

-Part 3-
A Larger World

-Emily-

The sand beneath my body juxtaposed itself; course one moment and smooth the next. Course, then smooth. Harsh and comforting. Rugged, soft. Push and pull. Give and take. Like waves ebbing and flowing, saturating the shore on which I lay, soaking the rags covering my sea-swept remains. The salt stung my wounds... stung my eyes at how far from home I found myself. My bones and muscles, every sinew holding me together refused to lift me from my shallow grave upon the beach.

My placement started innocently enough with I and my shipmates serving the midnight watch. We played liars dice by lamplight, the liquified whale blubber burning its golden glow against the Pacific's peaceless darkness. Clouds blew silently overhead, masking the sky. Even if the moon had been visible, it never could have penetrated the miasma blanketing the shapeless void far beneath the main deck. Five of us played, gambling onboard duties with every passing round. Deck swabbing, rigging repair, barnacle scraping, cooking... didn't matter what chore got named, each of us had a task we hated. The boatswain made each man's labor a hell, a taskmaster of considerable power. Young Billy Rose swore the man was one of Pharaoh's slave drivers immortalized to torture men until the second coming of Christ.

None of us were inclined to argue. But we were of a mind to mutiny. At least against that beast of a man the captain called Mister Jack Griggs. We jested about merely throwing Griggs overboard in the middle of the night; we'd gladly spend the rest of the voyage in the brig if it meant a reprieve from our torment.

Oh, if only we knew how to accurately describe torment in those days!

We continued playing, selling the souls of our commissions until four bells. We started nearly an hour and a half before, picking up and tossing the dotted ivory cubes without consideration for our responsibilities. We neglected our duties to our peril and to my ever-lasting shame.

Oh, how I betrayed my brothers as I looked at my dice and found snake eyes.

Peter.

The voice – was it a voice or had I hallucinated the intonation – lilted on the gentle easterly blowing 'cross the deck. The sails fluttered like ghosts, their trimmed lengths and retracted yardarms stirring up nervous tensions and superstitions amongst the lot of us. Isaac Mumford, one of our best harpooners, stood and stretched his back. He had the most seasons on the water. His trained eye earned him a special place with the captain whom he served on five previous voyages. He could spot a cow from a thousand yards off and a fathom deep, and he'd be one of the first men in the longboat with projectile in hand. Earlier that day he buried his spear halfway up the steel head into the sperm whale's hide. The attack stopped the animal in the water, crimson mixing furiously with dark blue. It took four boats to haul the massive carcass for tonguing aboard the ship.

I stood, responding to my name, the word simultaneously sweet and dangerous; I wanted none of it and all of it. I saw nothing on the blackened horizon and sat down to continue playing. But a shudder rocked the starboard hull, sending me sprawling across the deck.

"What was that," Billy Rose asked.

His voice quavered with alarm.

"Was that the Bull," James Buck asked.

Every sailor onboard heard the tale of the Essex. Some believed the stories to be rumors conjuring superstition. Others genuinely believed the account of a devil-worthy whale capable of downing a two hundred thirty-nine-ton vessel in a single blow. I experienced a bull's charge against a whaler before and what hit us used far more force than I ever experienced on the sea four years earlier. I stood again and looked towards the water at the base of the hull, finding nothing.

Another strike hit us, rousing more of the crew. Several of my brothers ran to port, staring at the shallows surrounding the atoll near which we anchored. Again, they found nothing; no large whale could navigate those waters so deftly and hit us with that kind of power while having no room to properly maneuver. A smaller whale might have better luck but they never bore the strength to do to us what happened on that fateful night.

"Hoist anchor," the boatswain commanded, echoing the captain's orders.

I immediately jumped to task, helping my mates raise the heavy iron chain from the chop stirring 'round the ship. We worked steadily and got moving into deeper water, getting away from the threat. But our victory was temporary as something large, heavy, and angry slammed into the port side. The screams of terrified men and shrieks of splintering timber echoed in my ears. Howling winds suddenly descended in the form of a squall, torrential rains battering us from all sides as whatever attacked us drove in from starboard, threatening to capsize the ship. Another strike from aft shattered the rudder, sending the pilot toppling to the deck. Another hammering broke the mainmast, forcing it to drop from its base and fall like a tree taken down by the axe-wielding woodsmen of the frontier. It collapsed to the deck; I watched it descend as if in slow motion, the destruction captivating and beautiful.

Peter.

I turned towards the safe, warm voice amid the cold calamity taking place around me.

"Look out, ye daft idiot," Jack Griggs shouted above the chaos.

I dodged just in time, hitting my forehead against the balustrade. I winced as I rolled to my side. But I had no time to recover. The broken mast crashed through the deck as the ship lurched hard to port. The anchor windlass broke free, slamming into me and sending me to my doom in the black ocean depths. Lightning flashed; thick fleshy columns rose from the water, wrapping themselves in a crushing hug around the hull. A gigantic disc-like eye – a burning sun of pure rage in the midnight abyss – stared at me... the last thing I saw as I sank into oblivion.

When I came to on shore, only a few small bits of debris littered the sandy landscape. Shards of decking dotted the beach, like the spent arrowheads of a long-forgotten war. I slowly lifted my head and studied the bleak coastline. The black-grey granules stuck to my face, the sea salt stinging the myriad cuts across my countenance. I looked for the bodies of my mates but instead found snaking lines of rigging saturated in death.

I stood and slowly trudged up the beach. I found myself shipwrecked upon the atoll near which the ship anchored. A dense tropical jungle spread out before me, the lush trees towering overhead. I entered the foliage, searching for food and potable water; I needed nourishment. I refused to survive the onslaught at sea only to succumb to gut-gnawing starvation. My feet clumped into the dank soil between the roots, sinking a quarter inch as the moisture-laden particles depressed under my weight. The sultry humidity pressed in on me, forcing sweat from my pores in bold rivulets of perspiration. The droplets beaded from my brow as I trekked further inland.

Nearly fifty paces into the trees, I noticed the landscape's slope change. It ceased its gentle uphill climb and steadily angled downward towards the island's interior. I caught glimpses of black through the branches, traces of water trapped at the atoll's center by the ring of earth. The wind blowing across the island brought with it thick curtains of grey-black smoke smelling of ash and the unmistakable odor of sulfur. The further inland I moved, the less I heard the waves lapping against the shore. It was then I noticed another peculiarity: I heard no sounds of nature. No birds. No bugs. No beasts. I was alone on the island as far as I knew. The thought terrified me as much as it intrigued me.

What else might I discover on this desolate spit of land? If only I died instead of arriving on this accursed place.

The smoke's volume increased, obscuring my vision and clogging my respiration with its choking quality. I coughed and wheezed, trying to catch my breath on my downward walk until I was forced to stop and rest. I sat at the base of a tree, inhaling deeply to fill my weary lungs. My focused breathing helped little and I resorted to covering my nose and mouth with the tattered remains of my shirt to block the ash collecting in my nostrils. A fine layer of acrid silt covered the top of my tongue. It tasted like the slice of stale bread I ate as I started my watch the night... before? How long had it been since the ship was...

Peter!

The voice came more clearly than before. It definitely called my name, originating from the inland lake. I knew the speaker; I hadn't seen my sweet Emily since my departure from Boston Harbor a... how long had it been? A few months? A year? More?!? I immediately clambered downhill, dodging trees and roots in my race to my love. I rushed as quickly as my weakened body carried me. I tripped twice before finally breaking through the tree line. I stopped suddenly, gasping at the sight before me. The slope dropped in a sheer cliff descending into the atoll's central body of water. The lake's darkness covered the roiling heart of a volcanic crater. The bowl shape still burned with the earth's fiery power, causing the water to boil. Steam levitated off the surface while gasses and smoke vented from fissures in the rocky ledge circling the lake.

Beyond the vapors I spotted a stone walkway spanning the churning water. It led to a large, looming structure built of raw obsidian.

I gingerly migrated towards the bridge's shoreline access, crossing it with tentative steps. The volcanic stone upon which I tread shifted not as I applied the full of my weight. The porous surface felt slick under foot, posing a danger if I lost my balance and slid into the water. What might happen if I made contact with it; would I burn and boil to death or would I survive? I had no way of knowing and possessed no desire to explore the possibilities.

Midway across the lake, the surface vibrated a sonic resonance channeling from deep within the planet's bowels. The growling rumble shook me to the core like a monster calling out, terrifying its prey into fearful submission to its famished will. The reverberation – like the ship-shattering impacts – rattled my bones. I collapsed to the stone platform, trying to make myself as small as possible. I felt as weak and hopeless as I had floating in the oblivion while that giant eye locked its gaze upon me, its iris blazing with an eternal, unquenchable fury.

I cursed its horrifying beauty.

Peter!

The voice – *her* voice – carried along with the deafening roar. I waited until the cacophony ceased before standing and crossing to the temple-like ruins in the middle of the lake. I nearly cracked my head on the entrance's corner, narrowly missing. My dehydration-fueled delirium only waxed as I heard her calling out to me once more, prompting my obsession just enough to preserve my life before I accidentally killed myself.

The claustrophobic corridors twisted and turned in a confusing labyrinth, first turning left, then to the right before the tunnel double-backed upon itself. In my head, I pictured a gargantuan snake coiled in its burrow, waiting for its next victim to come to it. I wanted nothing to do with the danger, but I couldn't keep myself from pursuing my exploration. If she was here, a million questions filtered through my thoughts. Chief among them I wondered how she came to follow me out to the middle of the most vast stretch of ocean in the world. How had she found me on this lonely island? When did she get here?

As if to mirror the miring hypotheticals in my head, the temple's interior grew darker the further I moved from the opening. The internal atmosphere reminded me of the crypts beneath Boston; my father worked for a cemetery, spending his days burying the dead. The tunnels stank of damp earth and death, but something else mixed with the odor... something noxious with a tinge of salt... like rotting cod. It simultaneously revolted and attracted me. And then my nostrils flared against a scent I hadn't smelled since leaving port all those months ago: citrus flowers in bloom!

While I couldn't see in the blackness, I let my olfactory senses direct me. The soles of my feet scraped along the rough paving stones as I descended further into the abyss in which I found myself. I don't know how much time I spent wandering the maze, but I eventually saw a route open into a vaulted chamber akin to a cathedral. Giant support columns rose towards the ceiling, the octagonal surface blocking out all light except for the faint traces of sunset shining through an oculus in what must be the center of the roof. An array of dust-covered mirrors lined the walls, reflecting the sunlight during the day and providing a distracting obscurance of anything inside the chamber.

My eyes shifted in their sockets, studying every corner of the space. A ring of dark alcoves circled the central platform; ragged breathing and sniffing sobs came from them. But I ignored those sounds, drawn to the dais in the middle of the room. I spied a figure chained to the stones by her ankles and wrists, her face posed towards the floor. A dark grey robe of an unknown gauzy fabric covered her, its tattered edges frayed from wear. She looked weak as she prostrated in the temple's heart.

And then she looked up at me, her eyes locking with mine. They reflected a fiery glow coming from the departing sunlight, but I knew them. I knew the face. When she said my name, I knew her voice.

Emily!

I couldn't look away. I hadn't seen her in so long. I hadn't felt her warmth or her gentle hands upon my body. I blinked and was instantly transported to our modest apartment, the single bedroom home a humble beginning to a heartfelt romance. I remembered how unhappy she had been when I told her of my commission; how she cursed the day! We argued well into the night, but still we promised to uphold out marriage vows no matter how long I was away. I belonged to her. I was sworn to her in spirit and flesh.

"Emily? How are you here?!"

"I have been trapped here for ages," she replied, her voice moving me to tears.

I marveled at her retained beauty. It never failed despite the horrid condition in which she had been kept. Her ink-colored hair and amber eyes still as lustrous as I remembered.

"How? Who brought you here?"

I moved closer.

"He is gone now," Emily replied. "Free me so that I may leave this place."

"Gone? Where did he go? Will he come back?"

I stared up at the support columns; intricate, circular runes of an anonymous ancient tongue cut geometries through the stone blocks. The same message repeated in vertical statements down each side of the square structures. Faded murals on the walls depicted a bestial entity rising from the oceanic depths and consuming everything in sight.

I stood right in front of Emily, getting as close to her as I dared. Something inside my heart warned me not to approach; I couldn't describe what, but it told me to abandon the site and leave as quickly as I could. But how does a faithful husband abandon his wife in such an awful place?!? How could I leave my wife – my love – to the grim fate of being imprisoned forever in this... this...

I turned my attention to movement in my periphery. Something dark and thick wormed its way out of the shadows, wrapping around the furthest column, and retreated from view. A chittering gurgle echoed through the chamber, the guttural sound identical to the resonance vibrating the lake far above me.

"What was that?"

"Nothing, my love," Emily said. "You're thirsty. Come... drink."

I returned my attention to her, finding a trough of water ringing her prison. I knelt, sniffing the liquid; it smelled fresh. I leaned closer and Emily stepped back two paces, a soft squishing sound oozing across the stone perking my ears. I searched for the source only to be reminded of the delirium caused by my involuntary fast. Eventually, I drank, feeling my parched tongue respond favorably to the cool liquid.

"Hurry, my love," Emily cooed.

"Hurry?"

"You must release me so we may be together again."

"How do I free you?"

"Do you love me, Peter?"

"Yes, my dearest."

"Do you really love me?"

"You know I do."

"Oh, Peter... but you left me."

The reminder infuriated me. Emily knew how much we needed the income from the commission. We spent everything just to get married. Everything I ever did was to love her and do right by her. Why would she accuse me like this?!?

"How may I prove my love to you?"

That same slithering echoed 'round the room, snaking its way from one side to the other. It stopped only to be added to by a heavy grinding of something being pushed out of the shadowy recesses. Five forms – the bodies of men – emerged from the dark alcoves to my left. Another five emerged from my right. Still five more emerged from the alcoves behind Emily while a final set of six appeared in trios behind me on either side of the doorway. I recognized these men... they were those who survived the shipwreck. Among them I identified Jack Griggs, Billy Rose, and Captain Conway Richards... they hung from stone altars by their wrists, bruises and abrasions marking their battered bodies.

"My brothers!"

"They did this to me," Emily said, her voice as calm as the sea after a storm.

"What? How?!?"

"Does it matter?"

"Yes... they couldn't have done this... we've been at sea for months!"

"You never knew, but they took me captive in Boston, keeping me out of sight below decks until we arrived here last night."

"Don't listen, Peter Evans," Captain Richards bellowed, his voice feeble and tired. "Don't listen to that sea hag... it has nothing you need!"

"Shut up! That is my wife!!!"

"Listen to the captain," Griggs chimed in, his voice equally hoarse.

I studied my trussed-up comrades. They looked haggard, pale from a lack of sunlight and beards grown unkempt. The captain – stripped of his rank-honoring regalia – bore a wound on his left shoulder resembling a vicious bite. The wound pussed, the damaged tissue pink around the edges. Infection set in. Billy Rose looked practically starved while the others bore various levels of exposure, malnutrition and fatigue. Each man's wrists bore streaks of dried blood crusting to the skin below their restraints, which themselves appeared made from bone or some other chitinous substance.

How long had they been captive?

"Peter... Peter my love."

I returned my attention to Emily. The sunlight filtering through the oculus finally fell out of sight. The cast shadows bathed her in an unnatural gloom. Her silhouette looked larger than it should in the waning light. A bulbous amorphous form shifted in the dusk while the slithering echoed once more in the chamber's confines. The shape coalesced to fit Emily's femininity, its bleak gelatinousness hugging each curve and contour as if it hid its true nature the moment I looked over my shoulder at my long-lost wife.

"Emily?"

"Peter... do not listen to these men... they are liars."

"We are not," Captain Richards shouted. "We've been here for weeks, held hostage by this abomination!"

"Don't call her that!!!"

"You're being deceived by this devil, Mister Evans. Help us... free *us* and we can all escape."

"And what of Emily?"

"Don't sell your Christian soul for this forgery," another voice said.

I glanced at William Anderson, a seminarian turned fisherman.

"I gave my soul to my wife when we married. I have a promise to keep. I must protect her... I need to free her."

"Think, man," Griggs spat. "If we imprisoned her, who captured all of us?!"

I remembered pausing. My eyes focused on Emily's visage, tears streaking down my dirty face. I knew what needed to be done; I knew the sacrifice I needed to make, to give my life in place of another. I glanced down, spotting a jagged shard of black volcanic stone. I picked it up, holding it as I approached my love.

"What should I do?"

"Prove your love to me," she whispered, her voice as slithery as the movement meandering through the chamber.

"Don't be a fool," Richards shouted. "You're making a mistake!"

I held the shard to my wrist, readying myself for the bloody work ahead of me. I missed her so much. We had been apart for far too long and I *needed* to be with the one I cherished most. Nothing in this world or the next had the power to stop me.

"I will prove myself, my love."

"I know you will," Emily said.

I turned to face my captain and crew. Their weary faces surged with fear, anger, and confusion. The edge dug into my skin, cutting harshly. The warm trickle that followed the breaking pinch stung more than the wound itself.

"Listen to me, man," Richards said. "That isn't your wife, Evans... that *isn't* Emily."

"Yes it is. She's never looked so beautiful... so *alive*, Captain."

"Don't be deceived. She's a monster! Free us before you unleash a nightmare upon us all."

"Do you dream of your loved ones, Captain? Do you long to see your wife and children again?"

"Yes. Every man here dreams of going home."

I paused. I knew this was wrong. That I shouldn't be here. That we all should have died in the shipwreck. I knew Emily's presence couldn't be explained as anything more than my penance. But I was committed and I loved too deeply.

"Fuck your dreams!"

Richards' eyes widened more in pain than at my insubordination, staring down as the shard plunged deep into his chest. His last few heartbeats exsanguinated him, his blood drenching my hands and face.

"Don't pick at the seams of my heart. I am as much of a monster as she."

I ignored the fearful, flaccid screams of the men too impotent to save themselves from my work. I ignored the growing roar emanating from Emily's shackled body as her chains liquified; I had no way of determining if the sound came from her or the long-dormant hellmouth awakening beneath this *tomb*.

I slit twenty throats after cutting out the captain's heart. I turned to face my love, walking towards her with the shard digging fully into my wrists. I dropped to my knees, weak from exertion and blood loss. I waited for a long-forgotten kiss from her lips. Arms, thick and circular, enveloped my body in their crushing embrace. Tubular openings suctioned across my withered frame as my eyes beheld a wonderful and terrifying sight.

Emily took her true form; she looked so alive!

My mind raced with fleeting memories. Emily lay so beautiful, so still, on the morning I left port. She hadn't wanted me to go; we fought about it all night. She refused to see reason; I refused to cow to her devices upon my life. Until now when I proved myself.

But I believed too hard; it was just smoke, like the toxic vapors rising from the vents in the temple's masonry. I realized this too late as I connected with the two burning discs staring at me from the cephalopodic being now dropping its illusion. Emily was long gone, not taken away but given up by me. Not abandoned by my wanderlust, but destroyed, her throat slit by the same shard of bone China I brought with me to the atoll when I boarded the ship... the same blackened, gore-covered fragment in my hand now. I still felt my fingers – like the weight of the world – wrapping around her neck to undo my mistake, telling her to not succumb, but she refused to listen then too.

Cold arms wrapped lithely, squeezing the life from me as the tiny, beaklike mouths gnawed at my flesh. As they covered my head, I remembered seeing those fiery pupils last before the crushing darkness took me, staring embers of hell like the hot gates erupting beneath me. I was the monster... this was all I ever was.

I would be with Emily soon, held in one final embrace for the last time in this life.

-For Elise-

My grandmother told me about the *Grinsender Kobold*... how it snatched children from their parents' homes after using its innocent guise to hunt the ones so easily taken.

My parents took my sister and I to the circus, hoping to help us cheer up a year after the war - *the* War - ended. I was six, almost seven. I remember being enthralled with the idea of seeing lions and tigers because they were creatures of wonder, as mysterious as those Oma told me about when I was smaller.

I always hated her stories because they were terrifying. Most faery tales are happy, full of frivolity. Not Oma's.

As we approached the waiting tent on that rainy night, I paused and stared at the storm drain just thirty feet away. I didn't know why, but I sensed something *unnerving* radiating from that dark, narrow opening. Something lurking... watching... waiting.

"Hey," my father said putting his hand on my shoulder. "You alright, son?"

"Yeah, pop," I replied.

I looked up at him, staring into his eyes. They were world-weary, glazed over from the time he spent in France. But he's home now. He survived the freezing, famine-ridden trenches and everything that came with those horrors. A part of him didn't come home, but most of him did.

I hugged him. Tightly.

"C'mon," he said. "Let's go enjoy the show."

I followed him and we ran to catch up to mom, who held my sister in her arms as she waited for us.

We arrived early enough to get front row seats. This hadn't just been my very first circus, it was also my little sister's first circus. The parade of animals coming through the tent absolutely amazed her; she especially loved the horses wearing sequined halters and saddles, their riders performing acrobatic feats. She grew even more excited when the elephants entered the ring to perform a variety of tricks in synchronous coordination. While I was mesmerized by the big cats and their tamers, she was scared the moment they opened their toothy mouths and bellowed their fierce roars.

I didn't know why the lion was called the king of the jungle, because they aren't nearly as big as tigers.

The death-defying high wire performers were the closing act, but the ring master introduced a troupe of clowns to entertain the crowd while the stagehands helped the daredevils set up the rigging for the trapeze, tightrope, and the safety nets. The first few clowns made everyone laugh with their mostly silent slapstick. Cream pies to the face followed by getting sprayed with bottles of seltzer water are always a crowd pleaser.

I counted a total of eight clowns in the troupe, studying their ridiculous costumes. Each wore some form of oversized clothing disguising how tall or how strong or how graceful the performers were in real life. Their make-up consisted of white face paint touched up with varying shades of reds, blues, oranges, and greens and they marked themselves with differing patterns. No one clown wore the same face.

I gleefully watched as one by one each of the clowns approached the people sitting in the front of the audience. They eventually made their way towards where my family sat, getting right into our faces. A gaggle of grinning visages rushed in comical movements; they moved so fast and approached so frequently, reminding me of the time I found the massive wasp's nest out in the woods near my parent's house.

The rotted tree branch holding the nest dropped to the forest floor, right near where my father and I explored. It detonated into a buzzing swarm of anger and violence. I never saw him so scared... he collapsed to the ground and screamed for me to run away, but I couldn't and ended up getting stung nearly a dozen times before he came to his senses and carried me home.

The memory made me flinch as the painted smiles kept getting closer and closer. Each forced expression of mirth loomed uncomfortably close, forming a repeated jumble of faces approaching over and over and over again until a new face appeared from the center of the group. I hadn't seen this one before... or maybe I missed it and lost the performer in the mix.

Blood red lips curved into a wicked grin. Green markings covered the white base over his eyes and earlobes. Shaggy mouse gray hair hung in clumps over its head, dangling into a face so terrifying I wanted to get up from my seat and move as far from it as I could.

This one kept getting too close, equally crimson eyes staring fixedly on mine. That same unnerving distraction I experienced when I looked at the storm drain outside froze me in place. The world - the other clowns, the ring master, the lights, the band, and the crowd - all seemed to disappear as if there was nothing else in the tent except for me and this *kobold* as my Oma would call him.

I didn't even notice when he crossed over the metal railing and reached out for me where I sat between my parents, my sister sitting on my mom's lap. My sister's fearful scream and dad shouting, "Hey" finally shook the cobwebs from my head and remembered where I was.

"What the hell are ya doin," my father shouted at the clown.

The clown didn't say a word; it merely grunted - or had it growled - in response.

"C'mon," my father said. "I think we've had enough of the circus for one night."

I couldn't sleep that night. Rain usually soothes me, but not that night. Not ever again. It took me years to better understand why, to put a name to what prevented me from relaxing and getting the rest I needed, but I realized the clown from the circus haunted me.

It still haunts me now.

My parents owned the grandfather clock my Opa built when he was younger than my father; it ran so well my father wound his own pocket watch by it. It chimed every hour on the hour, waking me up in the middle of the night every time it struck midnight.

My parents put me to bed at eight that evening, but after three sets of chimes waking me up, I woke a fourth time but not because I heard the twelve tolls of the clock's internal bells. The creaking of my closet door forced me to sit up in bed, my pulse racing. I stared at the door, hidden in the hard shadows cast by the dim oil lamp sitting on my bedside table. I rubbed my eyes, clearing the gunk from their corners when I heard the door creak again. I couldn't tell at first, but it looked like it slowly swung open.

I reached for the lamp's knob, adding more light to the room as the creaking sounded again.

I anxiously climbed out of bed and walked over to the closet door. I studied it, noticing how ajar it looked. I pulled the door open just a bit, finding my dress clothes hanging alongside my winter coat. My parents stored a small box of items in the bottom corner, but it remained otherwise empty.

I closed the door and returned to bed. I settled in, pulling the blanket up to my neck. The lamp's dull warmth radiating against my face faded, leaving me in pure darkness.

But then the metallic scratch of the closet doorknob twisted in my ears and the wooden creak echoed for a *fourth* time, forcing me to sit up and stare at the door again.

I got up and quickly crossed a *third* of the room. I reached for the knob; the *second* my hand touched cold brass, the door burst to splinters as a *singular* grinning visage pinned me to the floor and loomed over me. Its toothy smile beamed, its fangs dripping with viscous saliva from within a blood-rimmed mouth. Its equally burning eyes bore into mine and its moppy, stringy pate dissolved to reveal a set of ridges and horns like the depictions of dybbuk Oma once claimed to see.

A sickly green hue tinged the skin as the face pressed closer to mine, the thin nose snorting and sniffing as it inhaled my terrified scent.

"Ich konnte dich vorher nicht erreichen, aber es macht dir nichts aus, nein," it said in a horrible grating voice.

I struggled, trying to fight it off as it dragged a long claw across my chest, scratching a mark into my skin. It took every effort to get my feet planted between its scaly stomach and my body; I kicked out but couldn't do much against the beast's sheer weight.

The thing holding me down cackled menacingly, stopping only when something unexpected happened. My bedroom door opened.

I looked up, hoping my father - my hero - stood in the doorway, ready to do battle with this monster. But it wasn't him.

"Hen-wee," she cooed, unable to pronounce her R's. "I had a bad-"

"Elise," I gasped.

"Nein... du wirst mich noch besser befriedigen," the creature hissed.

It planted a scraping kick into my ribs as it lunged for my sister.

I tried to stop it from getting to her, but I was too slow. It snatched her and bounded down the hallway, crashing through the window in the front room and out into the pouring rain.

The rain pours just like it did on the night my life changed forever. It's been twenty-one years. To the night.

But the location isn't the same.

Before, I was hunted inside my bedroom at my parents' house. It was the one place where I should have been safe. Where my *sister* should have been safe. I expected it to return, to barrel through my closet door and steal me away from my parents just like it did Elise.

"It's real," I remember overhearing my father say to my mother; she apparently refused to accept her mother-in-law's warnings about the creature hunting our family for generations.

It never returned and my family was never the same. My mother needed to be hospitalized, unable to withstand the broken heart left in the wake of my sister's abduction. My father suffered a broken heart too, but he withdrew into a bottle instead of into himself.

Me?

As soon as I was old enough, I traveled on my own to my Oma and Opa's homeland, following the clues from Oma's stories and the kobold tales of ancient folklore. I grew obsessed, learning its patterns, its behaviors until it brought me to this abandoned mine outside Erfurt.

The folklore claims creatures like the kobold were once faeries corrupted by dark magic and prefer hiding underground, specifically in caves.

The mine at the back of a massive quarry yawns like the storm drain from my childhood, but instead of me cowering at the dark doorway, I stalk towards it as I ignore the pelting rain.

"Geh oder ich fresse dich," I hear it hiss as I step inside.

"Du machst mir keine angst, Biest!"

The kobold remains silent as I move deeper into the mine. I know it senses me, its large ears catching every scrape of my boots on the stone floor. Its fiery eyes stare at me; I can't see it in the inky blackness except for those bloody, burning irises.

"You speak my language," a gravely voice echoes from the shadows. "I can speak yours, mein Freund."

A flash of lightning casts the tunnel in an arc of blinding white. I see the crimson grin flare against the kobold's sickly green face, sending a flash of memory of it pinning me to my bedroom floor through my mind. There is a hint of another emotion behind the grinning facade.

"I wasn't there to kill you," it says, its heavily accented English as harsh as the rock surrounding us. "I was there to collect you."

"Why?"

"A generational feud. I did the same to your Oma's sister. And her mother's brother. I tried collecting your father. I sensed him when he came to this land, but he was too old when I came for him. So I followed him and waited."

"For what?"

"For you."

"Here I am. Alone in the dark just like I was when you broke into my home."

"And now you break into mine?"

I stoop to match its crouched, contorted height. We are eye-to-eye now, staring at each other, only a foot separating us.

I realize the emotion it hides from me. It's fear. The damned thing is frightened... terrified even... of what? Me? Why?

I think back to all of the stories Oma told about the kobold. It attacked children, the weak and helpless and defenseless. It avoided going after my father because he was an adult. I instantly remember something my father taught me when older boys beat me up at school: the weak prey on the weaker.

I realize the kobold is nothing more than a...

"Coward," I say.

"What did you call me?!?"

"Du bist ein Feigling," I say in German.

"Don't," it barks.

The sound travels like an explosion through the mine.

"You think I'm scared of you," I challenge.

"Just like you were twenty-one years ago," it says. "Just like when you were a child."

It's goading me, trying to distract me and get me off balance.

"Yes," it hisses, elongating the single word. "*Just* like when you were a child... just like... *Elise*."

Another crack of lightning brightens the space and my fist flies forward, catching the kobold in its snout. It shrieks in pain and snarls back at me, its face pressing as close to mine as on that night.

"Leave and don't come back," it demands, turning away.

"No."

It faces me again, its eyes studying me.

"No?"

"Because I'm not the one who's afraid. I see it in your eyes. You can't do anything to me, because I'm not a child any longer."

"I said don't."

The warning is hollow, but I see it tense the slender talons on its fingertips.

"You won't hurt me because you're a coward."

"I said don't!!!"

It moves with blinding speed just as it had before. It lunges at me and I barely have enough time to react. It's not as big as it was before; it towered over me then, but I'm taller now. It's more comfortable in the enclosed space than I am, using the mine to its advantage as it tackles me and tries to claw my face.

I kick it off of me, my legs stronger than they were then. The force of my defense sends it careening off me and into the diagonal shaft leading deeper into the mine. Its screeches fade the further it falls, but I don't give it respite; I follow it down.

The drop to the bottom is quick. It's too dark to see so I turn on the flashlight I brought with me. Craggy grooves carve canyons along the rock walls but here and there I catch shining glints of raw ore left over when the workers abandoned the site.

"Bleib... bleib zurück," the kobold says, its tone pleading.

I see a cut on its shoulder, the edges of the wound sizzling.

A smile spreads across my face, one I hope is as menacing as the expression the kobold wore when it first attacked me back in America.

"You're not just a coward, you're a fool," I say.

"Was? Was meinst du?"

It wants to know what I mean.

"The mine... it's filled with iron."

Its eyes widen as it glances around at our subterranean surroundings.

"Ich werde dich töten," the kobold growls, but I know it's just as hollow as its warning up above.

"No," I say, picking up a loose metallic shard. "No, you won't."

43

The kobold launches itself bodily at me again, but I catch it across the palm of its hand with the shard. The wound immediately burns its flesh away. Its new posture belies its true cowardice as it backs towards a far wall.

I kick the kobold in the chest, knocking it back against the stone and forcing it to the ground. I kneel on top of it, pinning it as it once pinned me. I hold the shard for it to see. I consider destroying this beast, this once grinning goblin haunting my family line. But it wouldn't be enough.

"Bitte... bitte nicht."

"Nein," I say. "Sag ihren Namen."

I lean in, dragging the shard's edge across the kobold's chest and face.

"Eh," it shrieks. "Eh... lees..."

I use the shard to help anchor my climb out of the mine shaft, and I make it out with only a few scratches and bruises from the scuffle to keep the kobold pinned to the ground. The rain ceases, leaving a bright, clear day ahead.

I make the trek back to Erfurt, seeing the banners and bunting as I approach the city limits, the fabric as crimson as the smile I removed from the kobold's face.

I realize just how badly I need to return home. Germany isn't safe for an American with the last name of Aarons.

-...Long Enough-

"Detective, what do you think?"

The Nomad struck again. Six murder scenes spanning eleven months. I found myself failing my city. Under my watch, twenty-five people lost their lives to this psycho's warpath. The Feds already moved in, taking over jurisdiction. Their profilers quickly put together a detailed analysis; it looked thorough to say the least.

The Nomad's methodology looked textbook; all signs pointed to it. Based on the brutality of the murders, the *unsub* – the FBI's terminology – was male, even if bruising patterns indicated smaller hands. According to their typology, they classified the Nomad as "process-focused, with touches of thrill-seeking hedonism and power-seeking". Truth be told, I didn't care what the Behavioral Analysis Unit reported; people in my city were dying and the Nomad has been toying with me, goading me since day one.

I ruminated over my history with my enemy. I fought a war, and it all started nearly a year ago; the precinct received an anonymous tip near the end of February leading a pair of beat cops to a warehouse on the southern end of downtown. Inside, they found nine gangbangers dead, posed around a table as if playing cards. Each banger had bruising and fractured ribs as if they joined a fight club before getting shot in the head. A few weeks later, the same two officers who answered the call were found in a dumpster by a vagrant. The bodies showed signs of a similar beating, the GSW's centered right between the eyes as if these men received an execution.

At each of the scenes, one of the forensics analysts found notes addressed to me. The wording came off playful, treating everything like a game. I requested I hold onto the preserved originals. Lab techs analyzed them, finding an auburn hair on the second note three weeks after the first murders. I wasn't even a homicide detective; I worked traffic. After two troubling tours in Iraq, I wanted to handle simple cases. As an Army MP in Mosul, I got really good at tracking hit and runs. It hadn't been what I tested for on my ASVAB, but I was good at it. Those skills transferred well after I got home and in a city of half a million people, that allowed my skills to shine.

But homicide captain Rodger Bell wanted me as a consultant on the case. Since the Nomad targeted me, he thought I might provide insight into who the killer might be. I took it personally, which was what the bastard probably wanted. I found myself frequently going for late night walks to calm my wandering mind.

"Captain, why is he called the Nomad," I had asked upon joining the case.

"Forensics found tire treads at the crime scenes," Bell told me. "Nothing in the database other than make and model... '72 Chevy Nomad. There's also the fact that his targets seem unconnected and there's no connected location... he's moving around."

"There aren't many of those in the city," I said.

"No, there aren't," the captain replied. "Hopefully we'll catch this monster soon."

The FBI quickly took jurisdiction as the murders continued and more notes addressed to me rolled in. One had been in the pants pocket of the bum who found the dead cops. One had been tucked into the sock of a trio of college guys out in the park. One was found taped to the chest of a pair of hedge fund brokers; they were found posed playing basketball on the courts of an eastside park. Each crime scene displayed the same MO: each victim beaten by someone with severe fighting skills before getting shot between the eye. The college kids had been somewhat different as the victims had been hung by their ankles from a nearby tree with fishing wire.

Ballistics came back the same, too: Beretta M9. Based on the way these men – all victims male – had been beaten, the Nomad knew how to fight, possibly an indication of military training. The ballistics only added to a profile suggesting an inactive or former service member. The higher the body count, the more the Nomad wanted me to know all about him.

Now, I stood outside the most recent scene, reading over the sixth note in my collection. It still needed severe analysis by the lab, but it read like the others. Almost. The previous five notes had been addressed to me, used my name, and vaguely threatened me. But the sixth one changed the pattern.

I remember what they did to me!
You'll remember too! I'll kill your career like
you killed mine... and then I'll kill you.
You're next, partner! One week.

46

I pressed my tongue into my left cheek, digging out a clump of masticated dinner from my molars. Couldn't get it, so I reached in with my right index finger; the taste of the latex glove reminded me what I was doing as my saliva grazed the paper in my hands. Shit. Stupid move contaminating evidence. The Feds now had reason to drop me when they figured out what I did... they hadn't wanted me to consult after taking over, but it was the only way to get Captain Bell's cooperation, quickly migrating me from Traffic to Homicide to the FBI... temporarily, at least.

"Detective, what do you think," Agent Barbara Felder asked me.

Special Agent in Charge Felder always looked like she should be wearing a lab coat, asking patients how they felt about their feelings; she reminded me of the shrink who helped treat my PTSD at the VA after I returned from Iraq.

"Apparently, I'm the Nomad's next target," I said.

"That's... that's *new*," Felder exclaimed. "He's never *named* a victim before!"

No. The Nomad hadn't. In fact, all of his victims seemed randomly chosen; the fact each of the subsequent victims had themselves been the first to find each crime scene appeared to be the only connection. The cops found the dead bangers; the bum found the cops; and now, the eight gangbangers – rivals to the nine killed first – had been at the park when the two bankers had been found.

"Yes, it is," I said. "I want to use myself as bait... draw this bastard out."

"We need to analyze all of the evidence first," Felder said.

"We've got a week," I said. "The Nomad's given me a week to live."

"Then he's tripped himself up by naming you the next victim," one of the federal profilers said, eavesdropping on the conversation. "We may need to rethink the profile if he named you."

"We don't have to," I explained. "I was the one who found the bodies... this is the lobby of my apartment building."

"Oh, shit!"

"Yeah," I added. "I haven't been back here in days... maybe a week. There's got to be more to this than we're seeing."

"I think it's best if we head back to the field office and debrief while the lab techs do their thing."

"I'd rather–"

"I know what you'd rather do," Felder said, cutting me off. "But this new note gives us a better idea of what we're dealing with."

I relented. I found myself sitting in the conference room on the third floor of the FBI field office thirty minutes later. Every piece of evidence collected on the Nomad sat organized on the surface before Felder and me, each piece categorized according to the date of the murder scene. I poured over the photos, looking for clues. Questions plagued me. Why did the Nomad pick these victims? The number of deaths at each scene felt simultaneously random and not; I couldn't explain it, but I felt the answers staring me in the face. I looked at the data, running it through my head to see if maybe that played a key into the Nomad's methodology just to cool my nerves. Twenty-five victims and if the Nomad got what he wanted, I'd be number twenty-six in a week. The madman averaged a little over four kills per murder over eleven months. The average age of the victims was thirty-one, and I still couldn't make heads or tails of–

I picked up the victims' dossiers and began looking at the backgrounds of each man. The gang members hadn't been difficult to peg; all sixteen had priors ranging from B & E's, assault, murder, various drug-related charges, grand theft, and running guns.

"I read the newest note in your *collection*," Felder said. "Who was your partner?"

"I've never had one," I replied.

"Not even when you were an MP?"

"Duty was assigned; I worked with a variety of other MPs. Some more often than others, but nobody I ever called 'partner.'"

I returned my attention to the case as another agent handed a folder to Felder and left.

"You ever arrest anyone that ended up getting dishonorably discharged," Felder asked.

"Nope, why?"

"Nobody you arrested for murder?"

"I'm sure at some point... maybe," I replied. "But nobody I knew personally. I've forgotten a bunch of those old cases."

"That doesn't help much," Felder sighed.

I knew what she searched for; she looked for a deeper connection between the Nomad and me. I was doing the same thing, but I couldn't think of anyone I arrested in Iraq or stateside that would have had it out for me. And then I remembered something that I hadn't thought about in years.

"Wait," I said. "I remember one major crime I heard about on the base in Mosul. Base MPs investigated a group of privately contracted security operatives for rape, but then the mercs went missing. Bodies were found three months later beaten and nine millimeter slugs between their eyes."

"Were they from a Beretta M9," Felder asked.

"I don't know. I had already headed home with my unit," I replied.

"It looks like the Nomad may have known you in Iraq."

"Possibly, but why come after me? I'm a cop. I haven't... wait!"

I looked over the files on the two officers killed in the second murder; Internal Affairs had them under surveillance for the last month. I began looking at each of the victims in the order in which they took place. The Southsiders all had priors. The two cops were dirty, on the take from the Southsiders, informing them of possible raids. I looked at the bum; he had a prior too: accused of molesting a little girl but there hadn't been enough evidence to convict him. The college boys dealt Ecstasy to minors in the park and on campus and Rohypnol to other clients. The brokers' files had notes made by the SEC; investigation for embezzlement of clients' funds. And now the eight new gangbangers I found in my lobby; they ran the chop shop on the east side of town I had been investigating before the Nomad showed up.

"What did you find," Felder asked me.

"All of the victims have a criminal history," I replied.

"I'll be damned," Felder exclaimed, receiving a folder from yet another field agent.

This one she opened and read, and didn't immediately close it. She stepped out into the hall for a moment while I continued to obsess over the murders.

"Holy shit," Felder exclaimed, coming back into the conference room.

"What," I asked.

"We got another hit on the Nomad's DNA from the newest note... there's a perfect match."

"A match? Who is it?"

"No name yet; techs are running it now."

"Let's get the car ready," I said, putting down my collection of notes and the victims' photos.

Felder nodded and led me down the hall towards the elevator bank. She turned into a doorway; I followed. Rookie mistake because I found myself detained by two field agents pinning me face down to the stainless steel table of an interrogation room. They had me cuffed to the chair inside thirty seconds.

"What the fuck is this," I demanded.

"You aren't going anywhere," Felder said. "No more jumping place to place for you... *Nomad.*"

"I'm not the Nomad," I said.

"Then explain this," Felder shouted, slamming a set of pictures down in front of me.

She sifted through them. I caught sight of a picture of myself in my army fatigues in Iraq I held my standard issue M9 at a group of privately contracted security operatives. My eye twitched and the corner of my lip quivered. I saw another photo of me standing next to a beat-up, faded '72 Chevy station wagon. My grandfather restored it but never registered it before he passed.

"I thought it was strange how a traffic detective got caught up in all this," Felder said. "Took me weeks to convince the DOD to release your service record."

"What does that have to do with it," I demanded.

"You helped arrest the men who raped you in Mosul," Felder said, waving a psychological evaluation in front of my face. "You never told anyone what they did to you until after the army discharged you. And you never told anyone what you did to them... you blocked out the memory."

"Oh and what was that," I argued.

"Someone pulled strings and got these guys off, and you killed them and left their bodies in the desert before coming home."

Something flashed in my memory. I fought the quiver in my lip.

"No... that's not... no," I shouted.

"We found the same connection you did with your victims here," Felder continued. "All criminals. Your investigation of the car thefts led you to both gangs; the Southsiders inadvertently led you to their police informants... to the college kids who got their product from them... they sold it to the bum and the two bankers. They were all connected, bringing back your trauma... I'm guessing you snapped."

"If I'm the Nomad, then why would I target myself?!?"

"Textbook: to get yourself involved in the case... you wanted to recover your collection. The numbers of the victims were an anagram of your birthdate, the day you were raped in Mosul."

"My collection?"

Felder held up all six of the notes from the Nomad. I studied the handwriting. The block lettering didn't look like my handwriting until I noticed a flourish on the S's that looked disturbingly familiar. My eye twitched again.

"It can't be me," I protested weakly.

"Do you have an alibi for *each* of the murders," Felder asked.

I turned and looked at my reflection in the one-way surveillance window opposite where I sat. The long auburn hair tied into a ponytail looked disheveled. I honestly hadn't looked at myself in a while. I resembled a world-weary traveler, and as I took a deep breath, I felt like it.

"No, I don't," I said as I smiled.

I realized I didn't have to wander anymore, but my war wasn't over. Not yet.

"Detective Margot Moreno, I'm officially placing you under arrest for twenty-five acts of homicide," Felder sighed as she left the room.

Took them long enough.

-Thrill Ride-

The silenced handgun barely even whispered as it pumped a pair of rounds into the back of an American diplomat's skullcap. High-velocity blood splatter hit Mary across the chest and face. Her coveralls became stained with crimson, giving the khaki jumpsuit a rusted color in some places.

With the corpse fresh, Mary needed to get rid of as much evidence as she could. She glanced around the decrepit basement. An inactive coal furnace stood disheveled and corroded fifty feet north east of the center of the rectangular room. It would have been wonderful if she could have been able to burn the coveralls and corpse in the furnace, unfortunately in picking a rundown warehouse for a base of operations, nothing worked.

However, Mary came prepared. She immediately began to strip down the jumpsuit. Underneath, she clad her body in a black fleece long sleeve top, black leather pants, and a pair of knee-high black boots. It was a sexy, classy look entirely alien to the dank, musty environment she found herself in. With hasty, almost clumsy, movements, she began disposing of the evidence.

With the coveralls gone, she wadded them and placed them on the body. Next, she began rifling through a grey nylon duffel bag. From it, she removed a small squirt bottle of liquid kerosene, using it to thoroughly spray and douse the pile of flesh and cloth. She emptied the bottle, and added it to the pyre before thrusting her hands back into the bag.

Klik!!!

Flipping a switch and pressing hard on an arming button, Mary primed a remote controlled thermite grenade she had removed. She moved back over to where the dead man lay, and tucked the device into the wadded up jumpsuit. With the grenade in place and remote in her hand, she dropped her safetied gun into the duffel and began leaving the building. At the door, she detonated the thermite. Even at seventy-five feet away, Mary could feel the intense heat as the mixture of aluminum powder and iron oxide fused and burned. The aluminothermic combustion didn't react well to the enclosed spaces of the warehouse and the room temperature within, but as it reached its peak temperature of forty-five hundred degrees Fahrenheit, she knew it would do the job. She exited as quickly as she could.

Once outside, she heard a whispering thunder crack followed by a zing of a high-velocity bullet zipping by her ear and into the mortar behind her.

"Fuck!"

Mary ran for cover in the shadow of the building across from the warehouse. The narrow alleyway didn't provide much shelter. There were no overhangs of eaves to hide under. But, with the cover of night and being out of the sniper's direct line of sight, Mary hoped that she could get away without being spotted.

She recognized the sound that the rifle spat at her; the silenced voice of a Barrett M95 bolt-action rifle. The United States had been using them since 1995 whereas MI-6 had been using them since 2000. They were lethal guns; their range was twenty miles under the trained eye and patience of an expert. And given the fact that the CIA or NSA probably wouldn't be going after an assassin as insignificant as her, especially since she hadn't ever worked outside of Europe before, it was more than likely that whoever was on the rooftop was either another hitter or one of her own people.

At least they had been her people when she had been an agent. Mary had gone rogue nearly a year ago when she took a job that had nearly gotten her killed. But that's why she did what she did; it was all just a thrill ride, an adventurous brush with death that she kept coming back from. Mary hated the addiction, but the adrenaline rush was just too great. She craved it like a junky needing the next fix. It used to be a career of necessity; people needed killing. Mary had run out of necessity and now killed for a contract and a price.

"Who the hell are you," she yelled upwards, consciously aware that she was giving away her position.

There was no answer.

She drew the pistol from her duffel, removed the magazine, and counted the thirteen rounds in it as well as the one that was in the chamber. Mary locked the clip in place, and pressed the back of the gun to her forehead as she always did to calm her nerves.

Should be enough, she told herself.

Swearing inwardly, Mary began to silently sidestep to her right.

Thup!

The sniper round tore through the asphalt of the weathered alley. The shooter was right above her. Mary attempted to sidestep back to the left. Another bullet book-ended her position. The shooter was keeping her pinned.

"Fuck," she said, even more loudly than the first time.

She was getting simultaneously pissed off and scared.

So this is what it feels like to be on the receiving end of the scope, she thought.

Keeping a running count of how many bullets the sniper had fired, Mary forced herself to remember details about the gun being used against her. The M95 kept a five-round clip, and three shots had been fired.

She moved left again.

The sniper grazed her skin with the frictioned surface of a bullet, burning her slightly and tearing the fleece of her top. She bit back a yelp of pain as she felt warm blood seep slowly from the bullet's laceration. She moved right.

The last round clipped the asphalt, inspiring Mary to take off in a lung-burning sprint to her left. She exited the alley and into the open of a shutdown portion of London's Pier One. She could smell the clammy waters of the Thames more readily now.

A man came around the corner of another building. Mary almost ignored him until she saw a flash of light ignite a glint of gunmetal as he raised a sidearm. Mary aimed as if in slow motion and shot him through the throat. She didn't look back, but in her mind's eye, she could see the man drop to his knees and clutching his throat as the sniper she had left behind replaced a full clip into his weapon and chambered the first round.

Mary focused as she shot another MI-6 agent that peeked into view, then tumbled in a tucked roll as another high-velocity round bore into the pavement. A succession of three shots followed on her heels before she was able to find cover.

"What the hell do you want from me," she called out, nearly outmatched by a loud gust of wind coming off the river.

Another thunder crack replied, signaling that a tenth round had been expired, hitting the mortar in the wall near her. The sniper went through two clips; hitting her only once out of ten shots. Only ten percent accurate, but though the wound wasn't lethal, it was most certainly painful. The sniper could have easily killed her instead of playing that mind-fucking game of nerves and wills in the alley. One round hit her and nine missed, but only four of those misses were by accident. That gave the shooter a sixty percent accuracy rating. Either he was still green from training, or he was screwing with her. Mary assumed the latter, because even at sixty percent, he was no less dangerous.

"You're a liability, Mary."

The feminine voice reverberated out of the darkness of an alley no more than ten feet from where Mary hid. A woman walked out of the lightless corridor, and stood within arm's reach from the lone assassin. She wore a charcoal pantsuit. Her brunette bun looked like a silky, wicker helmet. Her gaunt features seemed more underfed than sickly. She was maybe twenty or twenty-five years older than Mary and gave the impression of some kind of prep school headmistress.

"Mother Mary," the woman cooed in a threateningly benign tone.

"Ellen," Mary responded in recognition of the agent who had once trained her.

Mary kept her gun at the ready even though she had dropped her aim.

Ellen was a woman on the prowl; like a hungry lioness stalking an impala, she moved closer to her former student. In a similar manner akin to a predator baring its teeth and growling, she grinned and drew a sidearm from a holster tucked in her back.

"You're a liability," Ellen said in a proper British accent.

"You said that already," Mary said, enforcing her Scottish brogue.

She knew Ellen was an elitist, stemming from a long line of ancestors that hated the Scots for one reason or another. Ellen's reason was far more personal, and after years of acquaintance, Mary still didn't understand why Ellen hated her so much. She had tried harder than anyone to learn the tools of the trade. Her only faults had been impatience and a disregard for authority.

"How am I a liability?"

"You know the ins and outs of MI-6," Ellen replied. "That puts any security program, routine, or detail in potential jeopardy."

"And that means what to me? None of the jobs I've taken have had anything to do with MI-6 or its people. None of them compromised British national security. You have nothing on me."

"What about that diplomat that you incinerated," Ellen asked. "He doesn't count?"

"Hardly," Mary retorted. "He was just some blighter from Washington who was selling American secrets to foreign nationals and potential terrorists. I did the yanks a favor. I've pretty much left the agency alone, even taking out targets that MI-6 couldn't legally snuff."

"And the agency thanks you for that," Ellen said, clicking her gun's safety off. "But the director thinks you're still a liability. You know too much, and we just can't risk it."

"No I'm not," Mary said. "You guys are just pissed because I moved on to a better job that doesn't have so much... red tape."

Ellen smirked and fondled the trigger of her weapon with her right index finger. Mary assumed that if Ellen ever did have a lover, she would treat the man in a similar fashion; like a cold hunk of metal.

"Been shagged lately, El," Mary asked, insult and offense fueling her words.

Ellen lost the smile, stopped fondling her weapon, and noticeably broke eye contact with Mary.

And for good reason, Mary thought as a scuffle behind her sparked her instincts and reflexes. It caused her to turn as another agent came at her.

In a single move, Mary grabbed him by the wrist and twisted his extremity behind his back. She placed the muzzle of her gun to his kidney, jabbing it into place as a reminder to him that his life was in her hands. She held his body as intimately close to hers as possible.

"Do you want to die," she whispered sweetly into the man's ear.

In another time and place, she could imagine this man being aroused by her lips being so close to his skin.

Nervously, the man shook his head.

"Then," Mary said so that Ellen could hear. "If I were you, I would suggest to your friends to back off."

"You have nowhere to go, Mary," Ellen said. "We can just back you into a corner."

"Ever see a wounded animal backed into a corner," Mary asked indignantly. "You press too much, they'll attack."

"You've only got two options, Mary. You let us take you in quietly or we put you down."

"It's that simple, El?"

Ellen sighed. This debate was tiresome, but a tactical ploy nonetheless. She knew Mary was only attempting to buy time, keeping her talking long enough to figure out a usable escape route.

"You can't escape me, Mary," Ellen said. "I taught you everything you know. I know every move you'll make, every safe house you'll go to. It's why the agency sent me. I know you better than you know yourself."

"You didn't teach me everything... Ma. Dah taught me some things you never did. But that's why you quit on me, isn't it? Because I wouldn't be that proper English lass you wanted me to be; too Scottish for your pure blood."

With a whisper, Mary pumped a bullet through the man's back. It pushed through his kidney and out his front, winging Ellen in the right shoulder.

The lone assassin turned and fled as the pair of agents dropped; Ellen clutching her wound with her left hand and bracing the bleeding man's gaping hole with the other.

"Code one," Ellen announced into her COM so that the remainder of her team would be aware. "Agents down. I repeat: agents down."

-Salvage-

29 JULY 2332 – 23:57 HRS Standard Sol Time

The dark void of space yawned eternally into nothingness. White and yellow dots of glowing light twinkled faintly over the velvety ink of the expanse. Nothing could be heard. Nothing could be seen. Except for a shuttle pod drifting lazily. The gunmetal grey manufacturing made the triangular craft look nearly invisible against the starry backdrop. The ship's aft thrusters – powered by a small fusion battery the size of a shoebox – ignited every eight hours, pushing the pod ever further on its trajectory back to the inner tract of the Sol System.

Over the course of time, it made its way from the planet Threshold-5, formerly KOI-947.01 in the Proxima Centauri system. The nearly four-and-a-quarter lightyear trip had taken some time even with the powerful sublight engines driving the shuttle pod back towards its planet of origin: Earth. Occasional bursts of compressed gas jetted out from lateral, dorsal, and ventral thrusters strategically positioned around the outer hull of the ship; each puff minutely adjusted the ship's course, repositioning it via autopilot with coordinates and commands preprogrammed years earlier during the vessel's construction. It passed by quasars, pulsars, and black holes; all of these rare galactic occurrences happened millions of kilometers away, silently ignoring the shuttle as it gently and steadily meandered about on its way back home.

It remained in such a state until the shadow of a larger vessel approached.

The deep space salvage trawler, *The Avarice*, had been cruising around at sublight nearly half a million kilometers outside Pluto's gravity well when its outboard sensor suite began detecting the shuttle pod. A series of pinging alerts began chiming from the computer system, telling the crew of the trawler that something existed just half a klick off the port bow. The automated system piloting the trawler immediately cut thrust and began negotiating its own pitch and yaw to align its hull with that of the shuttle. As the computer cycled the automated docking subroutines, extending an umbilicus from the rear of the cargo hold towards shuttle's port side hatch, the five-man crew of *The Avarice* began gearing up to board it.

Three men of varying age and two women in their early- to mid-twenties slid their tired, weary bodies into thick, heavy pressurized suits. The mud-brown and white suits consisted of a single piece jumpsuit used for EVA – extravehicular activities – with built-in magnetic boots and second skin gloves that allowed the crew to manipulate tools and tech with the same ease as if they weren't even wearing the gloves in the first place.

They slid in feet first, pulling the body and sleeves of the suit onto their bodies as they ducked momentarily under the collar. They sealed the front opening, making sure it didn't have any compromises before they each reached for the domed transparisteel helmets.

"What did we hit, Cap'n," the forty-five year old man with a shaved head and graying goatee asked.

"Didn't hit nothin', Dane," a black man with a British accent replied. "The computer picked up a flee floating out there in the black."

"Flea," the younger looking of the two women inquired, unfamiliar with the vernacular.

"Yeah, that's right! Simmons here ain't got no idea what a flea is," Dane cooed.

"Hey," Simmons said as she sealed up the front of her suit and reached for her helmet. I know what the hell a flea is, just haven't heard that term used in like forever."

"More like never," Chow – the other female crewmember replied. "I've got about five year on you and if I haven't heard it used on this rig, I know for a fact you haven't."

Simmons looked at Chow with a playfully perturbed glance before putting on her helmet and closing the seals on her collar to make sure her suit had been completely pressurized against the vacuum of space.

"Seriously, Captain," a young guy in his early twenties asked. "What did we lock onto?"

He looked fresh out of boot, hardly a grease stain on his skin and a neatly buzzed head. He didn't even look old enough to drive a car let alone order a beer.

Delroy Hannigan – the captain of *The Avarice* – looked at his rookie. Reese Mason had washed out of training for the Colonial Marines and needed a job to help support his family. Being a close friend of the Mason household, Hannigan decided to take the kid aboard his crew, offering to pay him his fair share provided the boy worked his bleedin' arse off. Reese promised and now here he was, five billion kilometers from his home on his very first salvage mission.

"Well, rook, we've locked on and just coupled with a life support escape pod. The slang is a 'flee'."

"Why call it a bug," Reese asked.

"It's old school military, rook," Simmons offered. "Pods like this are designed to escape and another word for escape is 'flee', f-l-e-e."

"Oh, that sounds like the buh-"

Reese's words got cut off in midsentence as he locked his helmet in place and began panicking, flailing his arms. Dane reached over and tapped the button on the side of the helmet to activate the suits comms and the breathing apparatus.

"Shit. This boy is going to get himself killed," Dane said.

"Cut him some slack," Chow said. "I heard you were more green than that when you first started."

"Nah, I've always been a scrapper," Dane replied.

"Except for that time you found a loo and thought it was the lost treasure of Atlantis," Hannigan said, poking the bear.

"Del, why?!?"

Laughter filtered through the suits' speakers as they headed for the airlock and the umbilicus leading over to the shuttle pod. The door cycled open and five crew members moved with heavy magnetic steps through the cylindrical passage. Hannigan led the way, followed by Simmons and Reese; Dane and Chow brought up the rear with Dane cycling the airlock to *The Avarice* closed. Once the pressure inside balanced, they continued moving towards the shuttle side. Their footsteps clomped heavily as the magnets in the soles of their boots stabilized them.

While the ship had an artificial gravity generator onboard, the umbilicus didn't have that kind of technology plugged into it, so the boots kept them from floating around aimlessly. Of the five of them, only Hannigan and Simmons had experience truly operating in Zero-G environments. Chow had almost finished her rating, but until she finished it, that limited the kind of salvage jobs they could take and who could work in what conditions.

"Simmons, cycle the airlock into the shuttle," Hannigan instructed.

"Cycling now, Cap," Simmons said.

She plugged in a portable touchscreen interface to an outlet on the outer hull of the shuttle. The moment the interface connected to the shuttle's onboard computer, the touchscreen lit up, processing the connection. When the keypad appeared, Simmons immediately began punching in the universal code used on all standard escape craft like the one to which they had attached themselves. The screen flashed red for a moment and then the keypad returned.

"What in the hell," Simmons exclaimed.

"What's wrong," Dane asked.

"The universal didn't work."

"Are you sure you hit the right sequence," Chow asked.

"Yeah, I'm sure," Simmons replied. "It's a simple sequence. Star-five-five-oh-seven-five-niner followed by a second star."

"Punch it in again," Hannigan ordered.

Simmons slowly and methodically dialed in the code sequence. Star. Five. Five. Seven. Zero. Nine. Star. She waited for a moment as the interface processed through the connection. Again, the screen flashed red for a few seconds before returning to the phosphorescent green and yellow of the digital keypad.

"I got nothin', Cap," Simmons said.

Hannigan took the interface from Simmons and had her recite the code to him slowly. He punched it in just as methodically as she had only to receive the same response. This time he noticed a message that popped up, replacing the keypad: Military Encoding. Access Code Not Recognized. United Global Alliance Error Number 6-2A12.

"What in the hell," Simmons exclaimed when she saw the message. "UGA? This ship is over twenty years old!!!"

"Alliance codes are old," Dane added. "I don't think anyone knows how to break them."

"Does your keypad have letters under the numbers," Reese asked.

Everyone turned to look at him. He paid no attention, fiddling with making an adjustment to his environmental suit. He was smaller than the suit, so it had a baggy look on him.

"Reese, you mind filling in the rest of us on what you're thinkin'," Hannigan said.

"Oh, right," Reese said, snapping to attention in that way that broadcasted he had been in boot camp. "When I was in basic, they had us training in all sorts of old UGA barracks and facilities for a number of reasons. They'd lock us in at night. A buddy of mind figured out how to hack the locks with a code."

"Do you remember what code he used," Chow asked.

"Why do you think I washed out of basic," Reese said, his grin lost behind a glare on his transparent helmet.

Simmons handed him the keypad. Reese took it, swiping the UGA error message away with two fingers. When the digital interface returned with the alpha-numeric keypad, he immediately began typing in a code: Alpha-two-three-six-mike-six-seven-star-foxtrot-three-four-seven-niner-hash-zero.

With a beep and chirp, the screen processed, went blank, and then flashed the two-decade-old UGA logo that split down the middle. The logo parted in half, the two pieces digitally moving to the far sides of the screen where they disappeared. A message in phosphorescent yellow-green block lettering took the logo's place; it welcomed them aboard the *UGA Swift Paw* shuttle craft. A flashing rectangular button with the word "open" blinked at Reese.

"Do I open it, Del," the boy asked.

"Yes, please," Hannigan replied.

Reese tapped the button on the screen interface and the airlock door gave a heavy *thunk* before the silent hiss of escaping atmosphere filled the umbilicus. None of the crew could hear it, but they could feel the change in air density pressing against the legs of their suits as the door slid vertically up as it opened.

"I thought this kid was gonna be a waste of space," Dane said. "Good job, kid!"

"Thanks," Reese marveled.

Hannigan led the team of scrappers through the aperture; they each took slow, tentative steps as they walked aboard the shuttle pod. As they entered the discovered vessel, sterile white lights winked on, bathing the gunmetal grey interior in a pale glow that made the spartan environment look like the inside of a hospital morgue. The internal space had been divided into four sections: the first had been a pilot's station near the airlock door, the second had been a food prep area which looked like it hadn't been used. Ever. Chow checked the supplies in the galley, finding every foodstuff, utensil, and prep material still in original packaging, and much of the edible content still viable after twenty years.

"This feels like a tomb," Simmons commented as she crossed over to the next section, which had a bed-like counter centering inside an array of extendable instruments. "This med station hasn't been used either."

"What's back there," Hannigan asked, pointing to a darkened corner towards the aft near a maintenance locker.

The quintet panned wrist-mounted flashlights in the direction their captain indicated. In the corner, they found two smaller pods made of white polymer and transparisteel plating. The nearly cylinder-like pods almost resembled coffins.

"These are cryotubes," Dane said. "Haven't seen these used since the speed on sublight crafts was tripled."

"They still use them on really long deep space voyages," Chow said as she left the galley and approached the others. "Colony ships use them because it takes ten years in most cases to get to where the newest colonies are being built."

"Is there anybody inside," Reese asked.

Simmons walked over to the closest cryotube, wiping a layer of dust and moisture off the surface of the transparent lid. Shining her light at an angle, she caught the glimpse of two faces, both female. One had a bandage covering most of her head, her long brown hair obscured by white gauze stained with dark blood. The other, a blonde with an attractive face, didn't appear to be injured. Simmons tapped the readout display to check for signs of life; it responded by asking for an authentication code.

"Yes," she said. "Two women."

"Alright," Dane cheered. "That's my kinda cryotube!"

He and Reese gave each other a high five.

"Calm down," Hannigan instructed. "I'm sure it's nothing like that. What about the second tube, Simmons?"

Simmons walked over to the other cryotube, again wiping away dust and condensation. Inside, she saw the face of a man; he had pale skin, chiseled features, and a bald head. He looked strong too, his body still fit after nearly two decades on ice.

"A man," she said. "He's alone."

"Three escapees in two cryotubes," Hannigan commented. "Where are these people coming from? Simmons, you and Reese check the flight recorder and look for a manifest or some other kind of log entry. Chow, how are the foodstuffs?"

"In great condition, Captain," Chow replied.

"Gather those up along with any medical supplies you can find. Dane and I will look for spare parts, power cells, and weapons we might be able to salvage. Simmons, if you can deactivate whatever autopilot program this thing has so that we can tow it into our-"

The electronic display on the second cryotube winked on, the glow a deep amber color.

"What did you do," Dane asked Simmons.

"Nothing," Simmons said. "I never touched a damn thing!"

The yellow light coming from the tube's controls began blinking slowly at first, and then it began to speed up. It flashed faster and faster, alternating between the yellow and a bright green color similar to the keypad interface Simmons and Reese used to access the airlock. Dane pulled a handgun from the cargo pocket on the right leg of his environmental suit but Hannigan motioned for him to lower the weapon. When the display finished flashing, it took on a solid green color.

"Cryosleep disengaged," a disembodied female voice announced. "Time in cryostasis twenty years, seven months, three days, thirteen hours, and two-point-five minutes."

"Shit," Simmons exclaimed.

"What," Reese asked.

"That's just a long-ass time to be in cryo," Chow answered him.

The crew of *The Avarice* waited but nothing happened. The display remained green, but other than that, the canopy of the cryotube never unlocked or opened, and the occupant inside never stirred.

"Do ya think he's still alive in there," Dane asked.

"He looked fine to me," Simmons said. "But if the first two was any indication, I wouldn't have been able to check vitals because it would have asked for an authentication code too."

They remained silent. Only the electric hum of the ship's primary life support functions and power filled the space. They could feel the vibrations through their suits.

"Alright," Hannigan said. "You all know your responsibilities. Let's get going."

Twenty minutes later, all five members were back aboard *The Avarice*, stowing everything they collected in the ship's cargo hold. Chow had the foodstuffs packed away in *The Avarice's* galley and she had the medical supplies – which consisted of a lot of really high-quality pain killers, artificial skin generators, and antibiotics – stored in refrigerated crates. Many of the items had a rather high value; one of the pain meds – of which she found fifteen injectors – sold on the black market for nearly fifty thousand credits.

There hadn't been many spare parts, but Hannigan and Dane found a sizable cache of weapons, including two different kinds of assault rifles, handguns, grenades and explosive ordnance, and battle armor. They also found two full crates of ammunition to go along with every type of weapon they encountered.

Reese took the digital files he and Simmons recovered from the control console while Simmons began linking up a remote access to disengage the umbilicus and pilot the shuttle pod into the cargo hold. Except the computer systems refused to let her have access. She even tried using the hack sequence Reese had used on the airlock, but it didn't work. Simmons continued to work as Hannigan began his debrief of his crew inside the cockpit of *The Avarice*.

"Alright," he said. "We have a pretty decent haul, folks. The medical supplies we got can fetch us a pretty hefty finder's fee as will he weapons; there are scores of collectors looking for UGA weapons given how rare and illegal they are. The food we could use ourselves."

"What are we gonna do about the bodies, Cap'n," Dane asked.

Hannigan pursed his lips and thought, trying decide how best to handle the discovery of the three occupants of the two cryotubes aboard the shuttle pod. At current, the shuttle remained tethered to *The Avarice* by the umbilicus despite Simmons' best efforts. On the one hand, he could just have her detach the tether and let the shuttle drift off into the void. But given the fact that the haul contained contraband in accordance with both the New British Empire and the East Asian Conglomerate, both governments owning close to eighty-five percent of Earth, it would be good to keep the shuttle in case they could leverage it as the source of everything his crew had salvaged.

"I don't know," he replied. "We don't know if they're alive or dead, and if they are alive, what their health status is. I want to get a read on their status before I make a decision."

"So are we heading back to Titan or are we staying on station for a spell," Chow asked.

"What's the closest heavenly body," Hannigan asked.

A few keys were punched into the console.

"Based on orbits and easiest trajectories, Kerberos," Chow said.

"Any facilities active there at the moment," Hannigan asked.

Chow tapped in a new command.

"No," she said. "Last facility cleared out six months ago."

"Okay, then let's head their and fix ourselves into geo-synch."

"You got it, Cap."

Five hours later, *The Avarice* found itself in a geosynchronous orbit above Kerberos, one of the five satellites circling around Pluto. The dark-colored moon looked foreboding as the ship drifted behind its shadow. It made the atmosphere aboard the ship feel colder even if the interior had been climate controlled and set for a comfortable twenty-four degrees centigrade. The crew had been sleeping in shifts; Simmons – who had been up for the last thirty-six hours – slept in her bunk. Dane had fallen asleep the fastest, an empty beer bottle clutched loosely in his hand as he reclined on a couch on the ship's common deck. Hannigan sat in his quarters, cataloging everything they had pulled from the shuttle pod. He didn't catalog the weapons, however; better to not have the contraband logged in the event they got boarded on their way back to earth.

Reese sat with Chow in the cockpit. Chow sat at the controls, maintaining the geo-synch above the moon. Because of Pluto's bizarre gravity well, it didn't mix well with that of Kerberos. The computer couldn't accommodate for minute changes in the gravitational pull because it was an older system and she just needed to tap a few command keys to the controls. It felt tedious, but it gave her something to do while Reese reviewed the shuttle's flight recorder. It had required an access code but the hack he had used on the airlock seemed to be enough to give him access.

Because of the older model of the recording software, He had to process the information through *The Avarice's* computer before it could be played. While he waited for the process to be complete, which currently sat at sixty-three-point-seven percent, he scanned a digital log on the tablet that Simmons had used to access the flight recorder.

"Hey, Chow," he asked.

"Yeah, kid," Chow responded as she adjusted the ship's orbit for what felt like the millionth time.

"Are you familiar with something called Raven Squad," Reese asked.

"Nope. Sounds like some kind of military outfit. Probably mercs or something similar."

"Hmmm," Reese vocalized.

He went back to reading the print on the screen, chewing on the end of the stylus nervously. He seemed a little skittish about their haul; in fact, he looked like he had been anxious from the moment they found the bodies inside the cryotubes.

Chow sighed as she spun her chair around to face the rookie.

"What's bothering you, rook," she said, leaning towards him to show her interest.

"Nothing exactly," he said, not looking up from the data pad. "It's just this whole thing feels weird."

"Weird how?"

"Derelict escape shuttle drifting for over twenty years in deep space," Reese started.

"Escape pods *are* found all the time by salvage crews," Chow inserted.

"With three bodies possibly alive in cryostasis," Reese added.

"That happens too." Chow offered.

"With high-quality foodstuffs, medical supplies, and military grade weapons stored?"

"Well-"

"*And* high-level UGA encryption software from before the NBE-EAC-NPC breakout," Reese finished.

Chow paused for a moment, considering all the puzzle pieces he had just given her.

"What are you getting at," she finally asked after a few minutes of musing to herself.

It became Reese's turn to sigh.

"Like I said, it feels weird. I saw the guy in that cryotube when Simmons shined the light on him; he didn't look like a fugitive or a refugee. He looked like a soldier."

Chow thought for a minute before responding.

"Well, like I said, he could have been part of some mercenary outfit."

"I don't-"

Reese cut off as an alarm began beeping on the control console. Chow immediately swiveled her chair around to face the console, tapping a few keys to silence the alarm. The flashing indicator continued to wink on and off, but the klaxon had ceased.

"Captain, are you in the cargo hold," Chow spoke into the wrist communicator she wore.

A beat, then static came over the comm unit.

"Sitting in quarters now, Chow. What's up?"

"We've got movement in the hold."

"It could be Dane or Simmons," Hannigan replied.

"Simmons is in her bunk and I'm looking at Dane's *wúyòng* ass," Chow replied, reverting to Chinese for the profanity.

"English always, please," Hannigan requested. "We're registered with the NBE and you're almost a naturalized citizen."

"Right, right," Chow said, glancing at Reese.

"I'll go check it out," Hannigan said. "Activate cams to watch my back."

"I can send Reese," Chow offered.

"No, keep him there with you. We're sitting in the middle of a gravitational anomaly; it's expected that something might shift in there. Hannigan out."

The cargo hold of *The Avarice* had been bathed in darkness since the crew stowed everything they collected from the shuttle pod. Lights in the decking acted as guide posts for the clear walkways between the storage racks and the lockers organized around the massive vault. The access to the hold sat directly across the space from the airlock leading to the umbilicus.

As Hannigan walked in, he activated a light panel; if something had come loose or had been moving around, he wanted to be able to see it clearly. Walking halfway into the hold, Hannigan spun a three-hundred-sixty-degree circle, looking for anything that seemed out of place or askew. From this vantage point, he could see the entire hold. It wasn't very big, barely larger than forty-six square meter apartment back on earth.

As he made his second spin, something caught his attention, something that should not be the way he found it. The airlock separating the hold from the umbilicus had been left ajar. He had been the last person coming back aboard *he Avarice* and he knew for a fact that he had secured it. He didn't worry about a lack of pressurization; the air recyclers pumped fresh O2 into the umbilicus and whatever ship it had been attached to, and the shuttle pod had its own atmosphere in order to keep the occupants of the cryotubes alive.

Peeking his head inside the open airlock, he noticed that the lights inside hadn't turned off and the hatch on the far side – the one leading into the shuttle itself – had also been left ajar. Stepping into the umbilicus, Hannigan let the lack of gravity take hold of him and he pushed off, floating the three meter distance to the shuttle. He boarded the foreign craft, finding that it had its own gravity generator. Cautiously, he looked around the shuttle; the space slightly smaller than his own cargo hold looked the same as it had when he and his crew disembarked with the salvage.

Except, that is, for one clear detail: the cryotube housing the bald man was now open.

"Chow," Hannigan said, lifting his left wrist to his face. "Chow, come in... do you copy, over?"

"Chow here, Captain," the familiar female voice said. "What's up? Where did you go? I can't see you on the cams."

"I'm on the shuttle," Hannigan replied.

"The shuttle?!"

"The airlock was breached on both sides of the umbilicus," the captain said. "Are you seeing any movement in the cargo hold at all?"

"No. Why?"

"No. Why?"

"Because... -*bzzzrt*- open."

"Say again," Chow requested into her wrist comm. "What's open?"

"Ker-to... -*bzzzrt*-"

"Where's that static coming from," Reese asked Chow.

"I don't know," Chow answered. "Stay here kid, and watch the monitors in case anything's in the hold. I'm going back to check on the captain.

Chow got up from her seat and walked at a quickened pace towards the aft of the ship. She roused Dane as she passed him by. The big lug of a scrapper got up lazily and began following her aft.

"Wait," Reese called out. "What do I do about our orbit if it decays?!"

Within just a few seconds, Dane and Chow found themselves in cargo hold as Hannigan dropped onto the decking from inside the umbilicus.

"Cap," Chow asked him.

"I'm fine," Hannigan said.

"You look spooked, Del," Dane observed.

"Yeah, I am. The second cryotube is open."

Both Chow and Dane gave their captain a disbelieving look. How could that be? The tube had been sealed shut, secured by an outdated military grade security code that they couldn't decipher. Not that any of them had the skills and experience necessary to hack such a system.

"Which of the bodies is awake," Chow asked. "The man or one of the women?"

"The man," Hannigan replied. "I think he's-"

He cut off in midsentence at the sound of something out of the corner of his eye that caught his attention.

"Dane? You have your sidearm," Hannigan asked.

"Yeah, why," Dane asked in return.

Hannigan pointed to the far corner of the hold; Chow and Dane followed the direction he indicated, their eyes training on the open locker. It had been one of the large crates that the two men brought on board from the shuttle. The door swung open, a handgun and two magazines missing from the crate.

"Oh, shit," Dane said just before a crashing sound caught their attention as something hit the decking.

"What was that," Chow asked in alarm.

"Don't know, but it sounded like it came from the galley," Hannigan replied.

The three crewmen headed into the galley, passing their own weapons lockers to get firearms. Hannigan hoped they wouldn't have to use them; even though the bulkheads were thick and wouldn't be punctured with small arms fire, he really didn't want to put any holes in his ship.

They rounded the corner of the corridor and turned into the galley. Upon initial inspection, it looked empty save for the cupboards looking ransacked. They tentatively took steps into the room, each taking roughly five paces before a hand reached out and grabbed Chow, pulling her back towards the corner. Dane and Hannigan turned, leveling their weapons only to find the man from the cryotube holding Chow in front of him like a hostage, his own hand holding the magnum pilfered from the weapons crate in the cargo hold.

"Where am I," the man asked coldly.

In most circumstances, a hostage situation liked this seemed frantic with the hostage taker acting impulsively. This situation felt like the polar opposite, the man from the cryotube coming off as calm and in control. In fact, he probably had all of the control in this situation. He didn't act irrationally, and he knew exactly who to shoot and in which order as he aimed his gun at Dane's forehead.

Hannigan holstered his own weapon; probably a stupid move, but he wanted to build a trust with the man.

"You are aboard my ship, the *NBE Avarice*," he said, holding his hands up to show that he wasn't a threat.

Something told him even if he held a gun to the man's face, he still wouldn't be a threat.

"I don't recognize the NBE," the man said.

"You and a lot of other people," Dane joked.

The man narrowed his eyes.

"I mean I'm unfamiliar with what it is," the man corrected.

"The NBE – the New British Empire – has been in power of most of Europe, Oceania, and North America for the last twenty years," Chow said as she struggled against the man's strength.

"What happened to the Alliance," the man asked.

"Sir, my name is Captain Delroy Hannigan," Hannigan said. "You've been out her in space for close to twenty-one years. We are a salvage ship. Our computer picked up on the signal emitted by your shuttle. We docked, we offloaded medical supplies and food-"

"And my weapons," the man said.

"Yes, those too," Hannigan replied. "Look, there's a lot to get you caught up on. If you put the gun down and let my crewman go, I'd be more than happy to sit down with you... maybe even over a beer."

The man considered the suggestion. Before he could come to a decision, Reese entered the galley with his data pad.

"Del, I heard you talking but I wasn't able to access the shuttle's-"

He cut off as he looked up and saw the man holding Chow, the magnum now leveled and pointed at *his* forehead.

"Oh, holy shit," Reese exclaimed.

Dane reacted, grabbing the man's gun hand and pushing it up towards the ceiling. The man reacted by kneeing Chow in the lower back and letting her go; he grabbed Dane's own gun hand and headbutted the larger man in the nose. He could feel the cartilage break and fresh warm blood gush from the nostrils. The man then wrapped his gun hand around the back of Dane's neck, keeping his free hand gripped around Dane's other wrist, using the leverage to pin Dane to the deck.

Kneeling on Dane's chest, he placed the barrel of the magnum to Dane's forehead and stripped the gun from his opponent's hand, bringing to bare on Reese.

"I'd make sure you don't draw your gun," the man told Hannigan.

"Wouldn't dream of it," Hannigan replied. "In fact, if you shot Dane, you'd probably be doin' me a favor. I'm thinking of spacin' him for what he just did."

"Del," Dane exclaimed.

The man mused over the original suggestion to sit down and talk.

"Alright. Let's talk," he said.

Five minutes later, the crew of *The Avarice* gathered in the common area between cockpit, the galley, and corridor to the bunks. They sat facing the man that had come out of the cryotube as he ate from a rehydrated cup of noodles, a large protein bar, and a cup of water.

"What year is it," the man asked between bites. "You said that I was drifting for a long time."

"It's 2332," Hannigan said. "Your former government, the Universal Global Alliance, doesn't exist on Earth anymore."

"Why not?"

"Geopolitical upset. A lot of people were unhappy with a one world centralized government," Simmons said in response.

"Come on! There was more than that," Dane said. "You probably weren't planetside, but I remember the Russ Pox in great detail. Survived them, in fact. That's how I got to be so pretty."

Dane indicated a set of pock marks scarring the left side of his face.

"Back up," the man said. "What are Russ Pox?"

"Huge pandemic," Simmons said. "Originated in the former United States. Killed nearly a hundred and fifty million people in North America, and nearly another two hundred million people in continental Europe. The British government figured out the pathology and started distributing the vaccine."

"Convenient," the man said. "So what's this new British... um?"

He took a drink of the water to saturate his arid throat.

"New British Empire," Hannigan said. "We call it the NBE or the Enbee for short. Covers all the holdings that Britain had about five hundred years ago or so."

"North America, Oceania, and Europe," the man said, echoing Chow's words from earlier.

"It also includes South Africa, the Caribbean, French Polynesia, and a few other small territories," Simmons added.

The man took a deep breath.

"What is the rest of Earth like," he asked, setting down his noodles and field stripping the magnum he had pulled from the crate.

The East Asian Conglomerate – my former government – covers the Korean Peninsula on down to Southeast Asia," Chow said. "Centralized government based out of Beijing with offices in Pyongyang, Phnom Pehn, Bangkok, and defunct offices in Tokyo, Kyoto, and Osaka."

"Why defunct," the man asked.

"They couldn't hold Japan. Yakuza began arming the people so the Chinese walled off the main archipelago and turned the country into a prison."

"What about the Middle East, Africa, South America," the man said.

"The Middle East, including Northern Africa and part of Eastern Europe, are in control of the New Persian Caliphate," Simmons replied. "A true Islamic State. If they had the firepower and military force, they'd try to take over the Enbee, but right now they won't and both governments are cozy with the EAC."

"Okay, so Northern Africa is under a religious theocracy. South Africa's controlled by the Brits. What about the rest of the continent?"

"Eastern black market trade," Hannigan said. "And Mexico down to Tiera del Fuego are the western black market run by the drug cartels."

The man paused the reconstruction of his magnum as he contemplated what *The Avarice's* crew shared with him. A lot had changed in the time he had been away. Too much had changed. A fossil from a version of Earth that no longer existed, he needed to figure out his place in this new world, but before he could do that, he needed to both find his way back to his home planet and find the man that left him in the position where he had to spend the last two decades secured away in cryostasis aboard a lost and forgotten shuttle pod.

"Can you answer a couple of questions for us," Hannigan asked.

"It's only fair," the man quipped.

"Who are you and why were you in that pod for the last twenty years?"

"Well, since there isn't anybody left alive to court martial me for divulging classified information," the man said.

-About the Author-

Garrett lives in Central California with his family and is the author of the fantasy series "The Archives of Icínq-Régn" as well as a book of original poetry. When he isn't writing, he serves his community by hosting free creative writing workshops at his local branch library.

Garrett is also a cohost of "War of the Stars – A Star Wars Podcast" and "Snack-ime" on Feast of Fandoms, and hosts "The Write Way", a video podcast on the GKJ Publishing YouTube channel, which is focused on providing top ten book recommendations, conducting author interviews, and offering creative writing tips.

The Archives of Icínq-Régn include:
Book 1, The Heirs of Menonias (978-0692513323)
Book 2, The Destiny of Dragons (978-0998563602)
Book 3, Rise of the Shadowkin (978-0998563619)
Book 4, Hadran Corvis of Farfell (978-0998563626)
Book 5, The Mantle of the Fatherless (978-0998563633)
The Lover, the Fighter, & the Philosopher (B00SPNDZOM)

www.ingramcontent.com/pod-product-compliance
Lightning Source LLC
Chambersburg PA
CBHW051312170626
46809CB00004B/1864